NK

To Maria Tippett, whose book
made this one possible – SVG

To the memory of my mother – PM

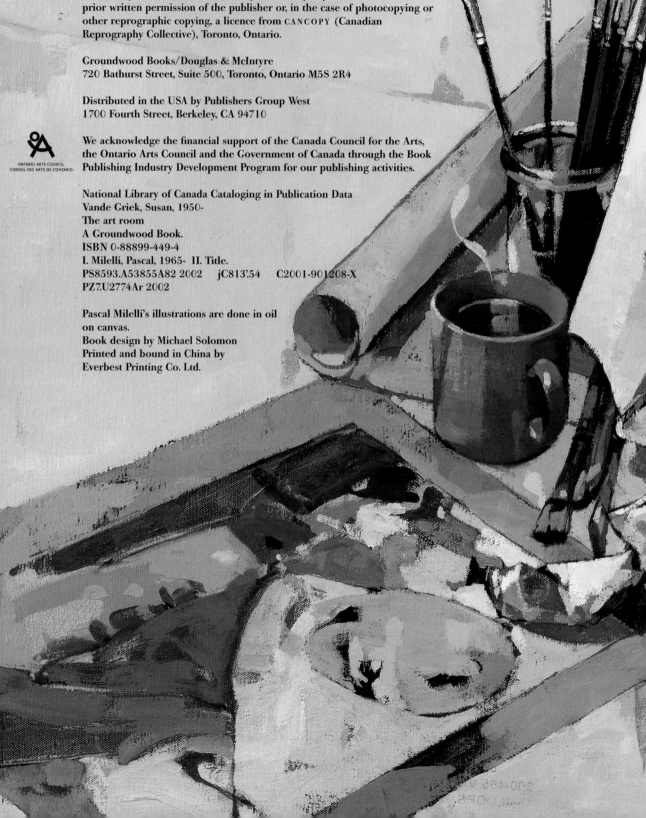

The text is inspired by a passage in Maria Tippett's book *Emily Carr: A Biography* (Oxford University Press, 1979).

Groundwood Books/Douglas & McIntyre
720 Bathurst Street, Suite 500, Toronto, Ontario M5S 2R4

Distributed in the USA by Publishers Group West
1700 Fourth Street, Berkeley, CA 94710

We acknowledge the financial support of the Canada Council for the Arts, the Ontario Arts Council and the Government of Canada through the Book Publishing Industry Development Program for our publishing activities.

ONTARIO ARTS COUNCIL
CONSEIL DES ARTS DE L'ONTARIO

National Library of Canada Cataloging in Publication Data
Vande Griek, Susan, 1950-
The art room
A Groundwood Book.
ISBN 0-88899-449-4
I. Milelli, Pascal, 1965- II. Title.
PS8593.A53855A82 2002   jC813'.54   C2001-901208-X
PZ7.U2774Ar 2002

Pascal Milelli's illustrations are done in oil on canvas.
Book design by Michael Solomon
Printed and bound in China by
Everbest Printing Co. Ltd.

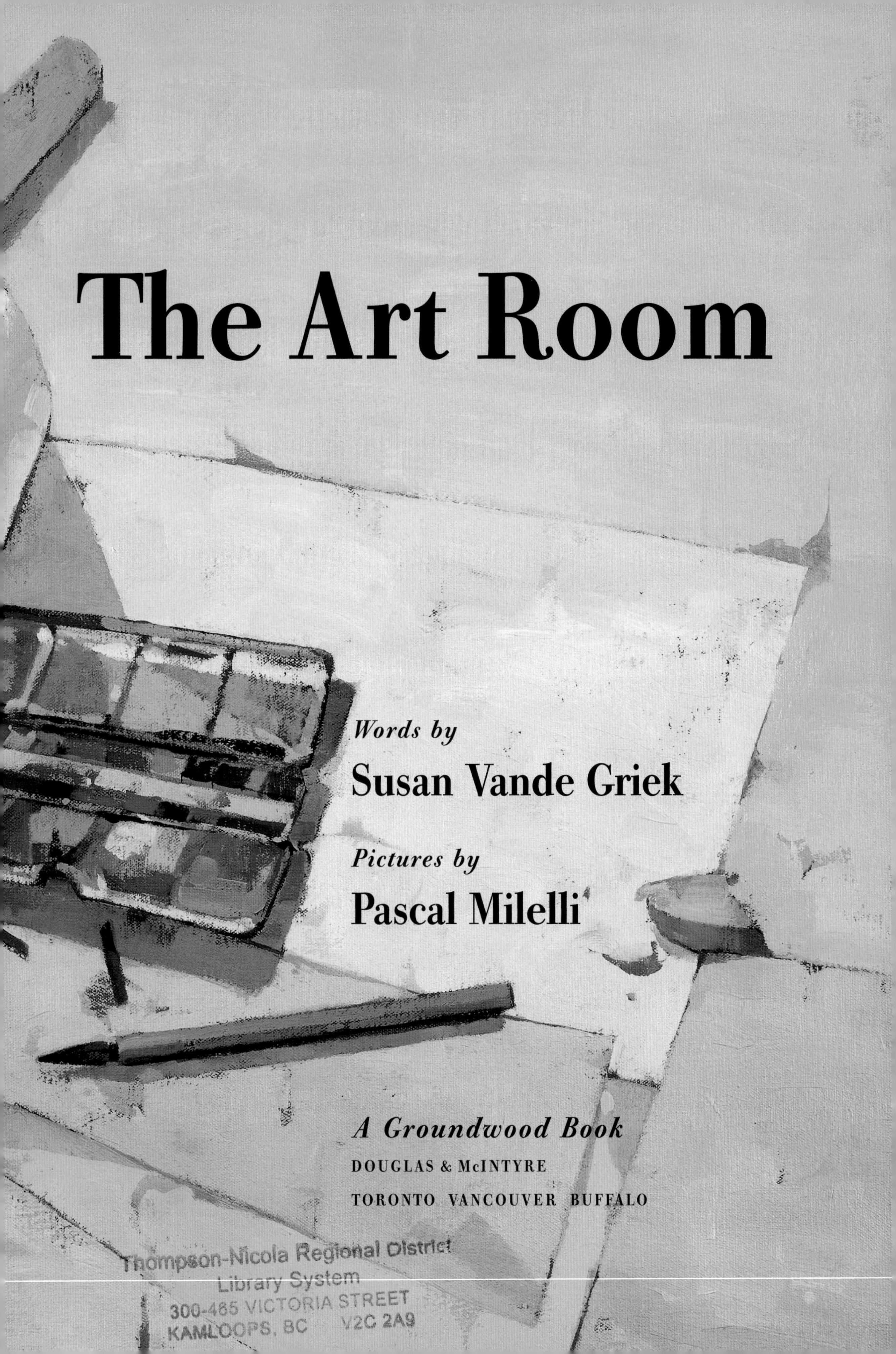

The Art Room

Words by

Susan Vande Griek

Pictures by

Pascal Milelli

A Groundwood Book
DOUGLAS & McINTYRE
TORONTO VANCOUVER BUFFALO

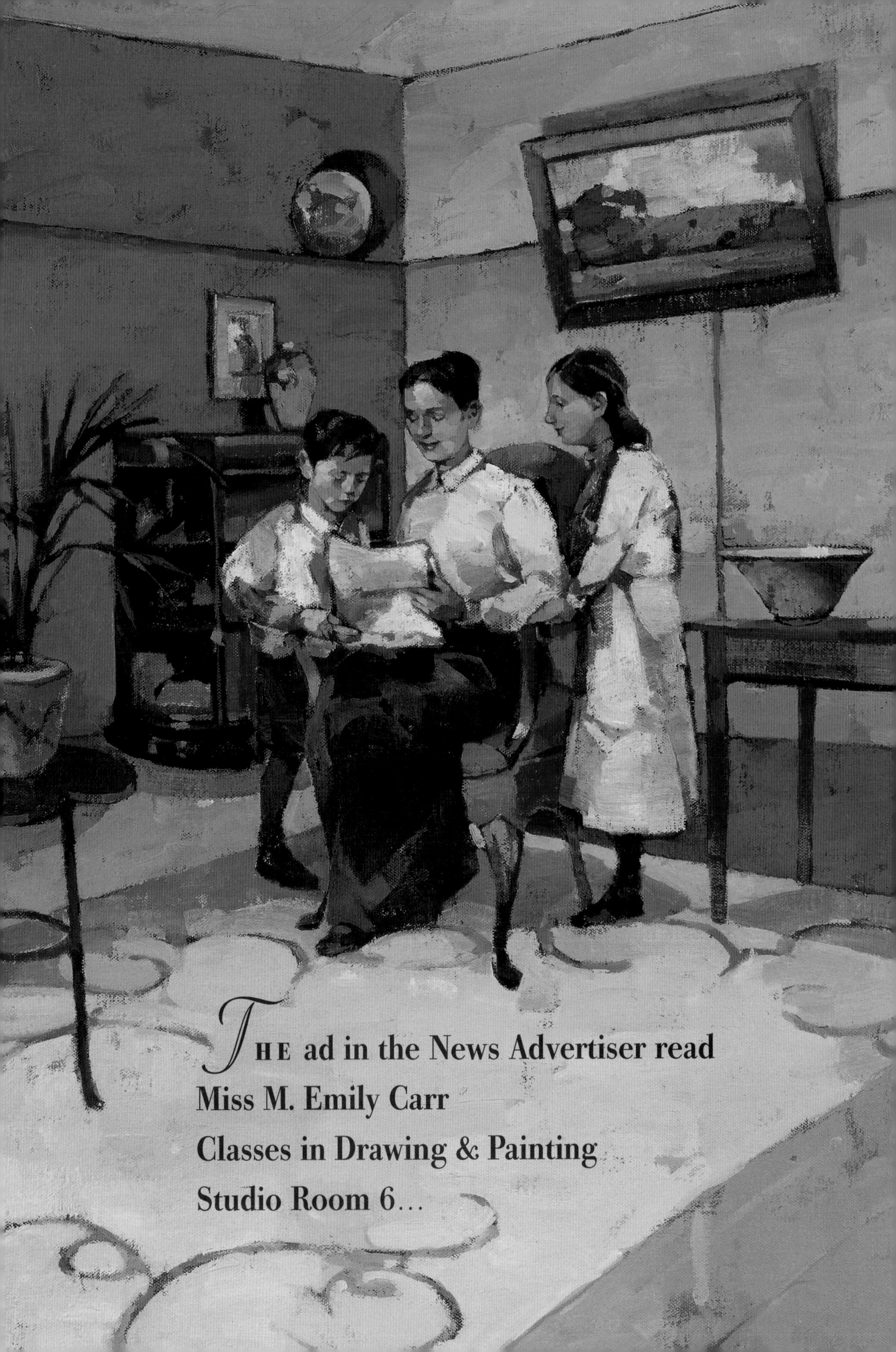

THE ad in the News Advertiser read
Miss M. Emily Carr
Classes in Drawing & Painting
Studio Room 6…

and so we came
and found
that new stone building
on Granville Street,

and we thundered up
those bare marble stairs,
past typewriters talking business
and tongues babbling news.

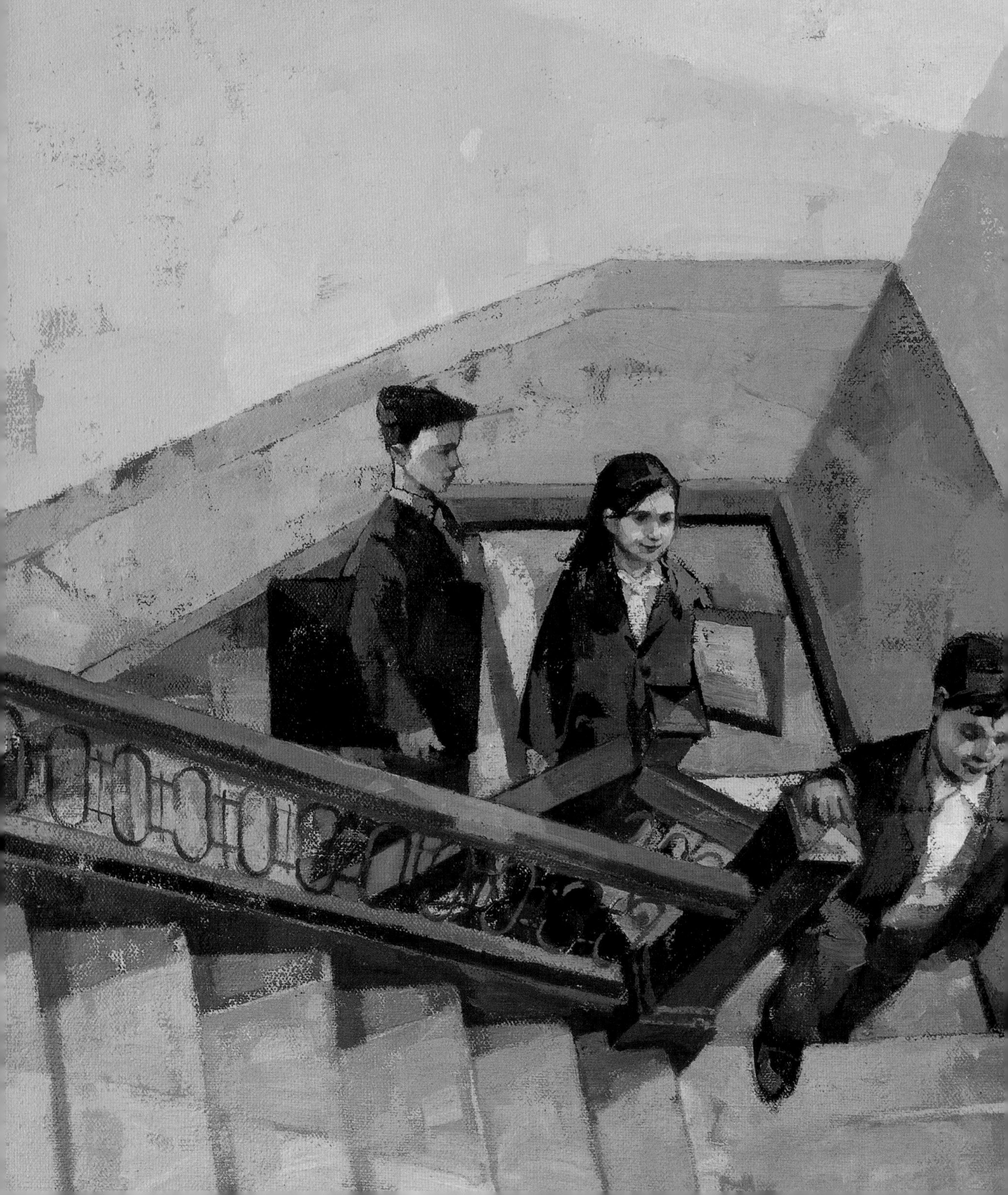

We threw our hellos
to Janitor John
and piled through the door
into the world of the art room,

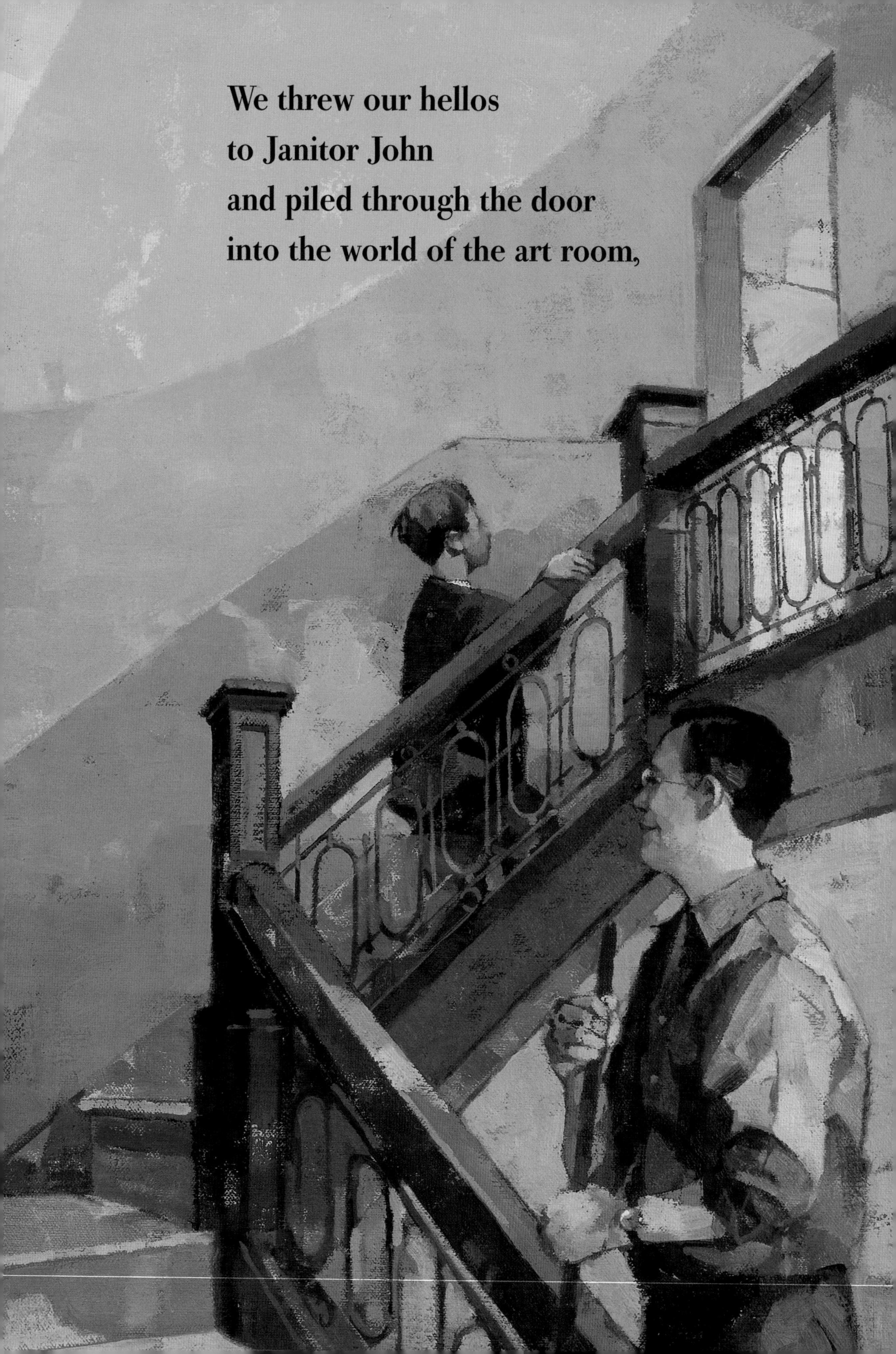

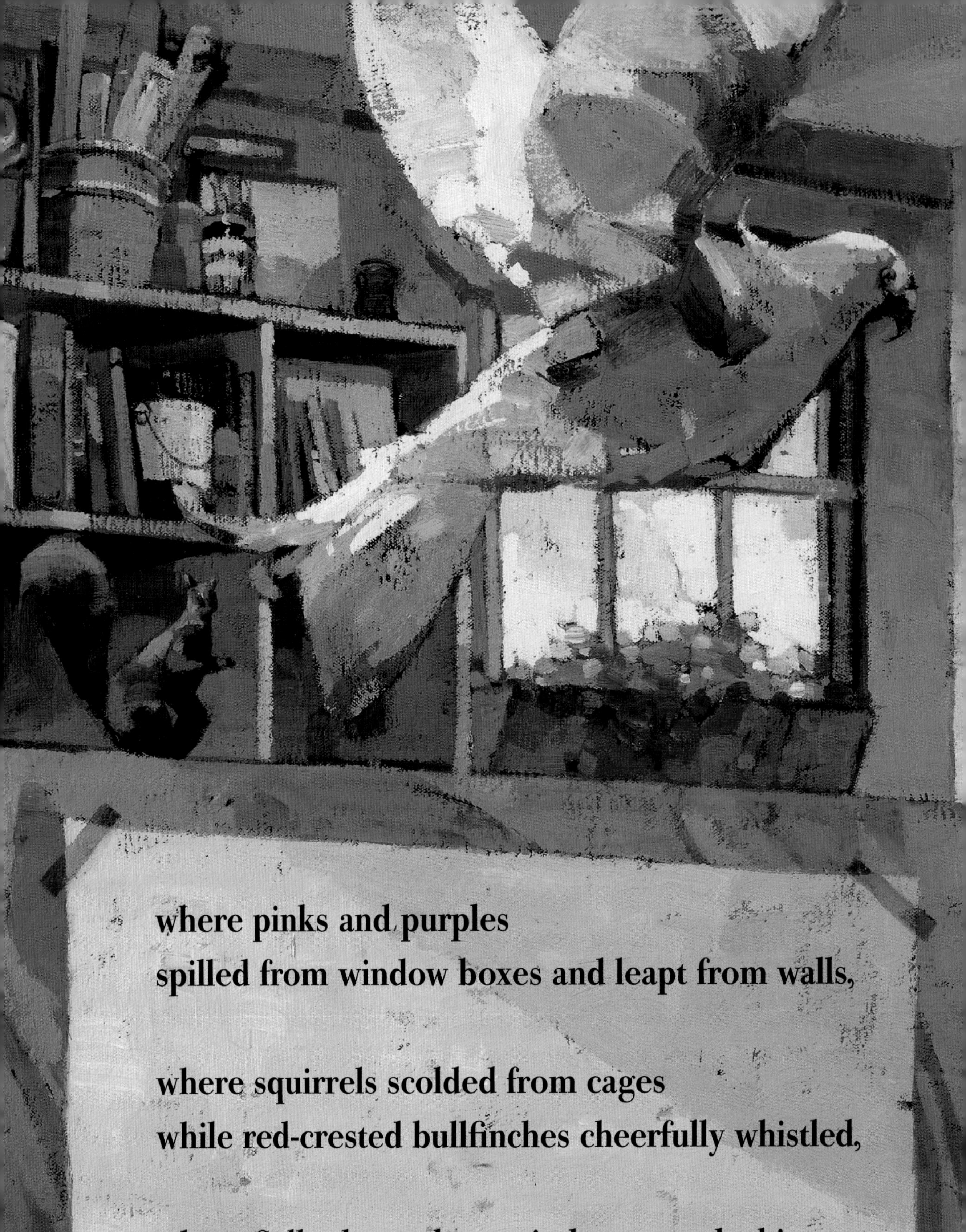

where pinks and purples
spilled from window boxes and leapt from walls,

where squirrels scolded from cages
while red-crested bullfinches cheerfully whistled,

where Sally the cockatoo, in lemon and white,
sailed crazily round the room

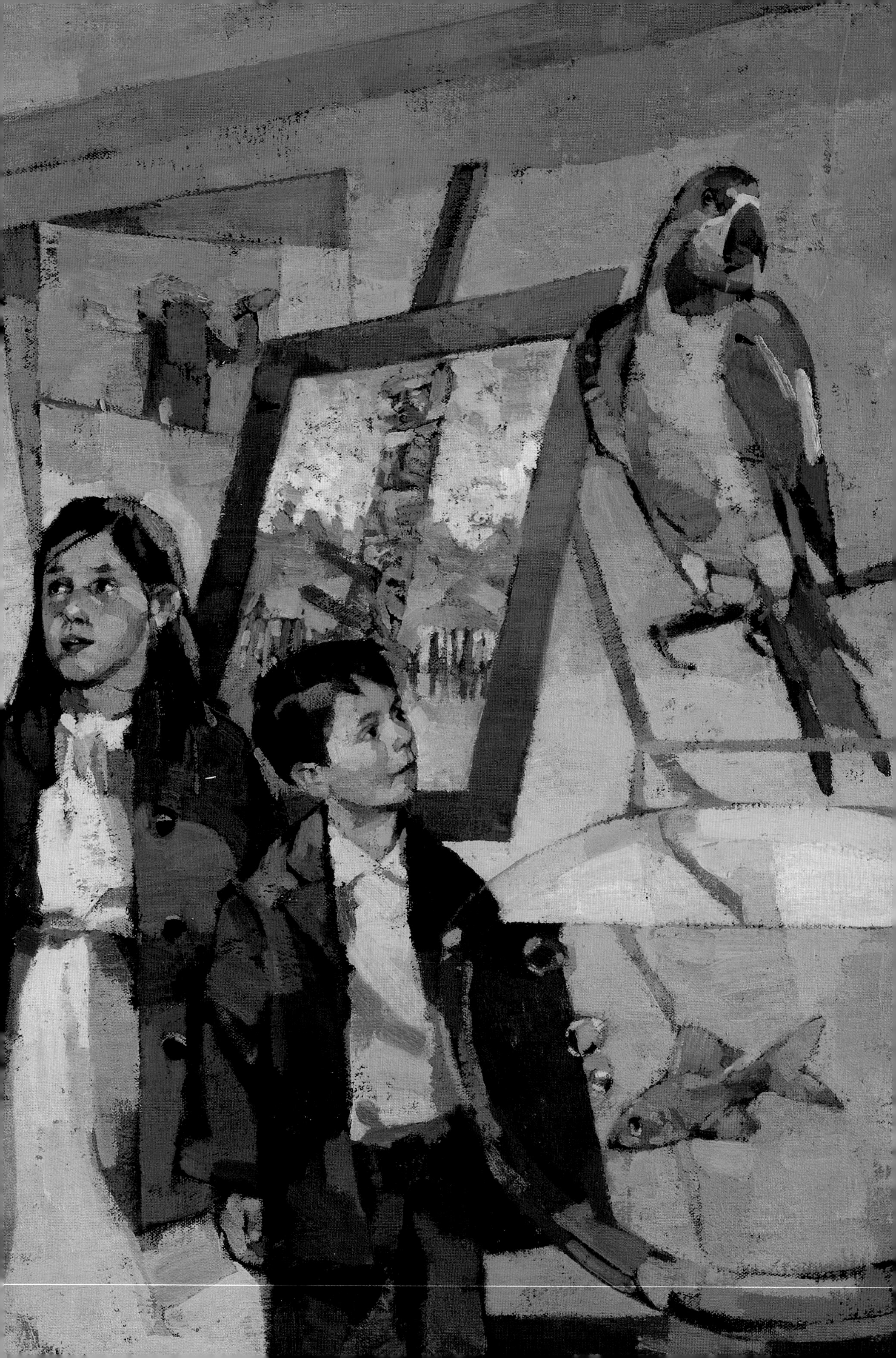

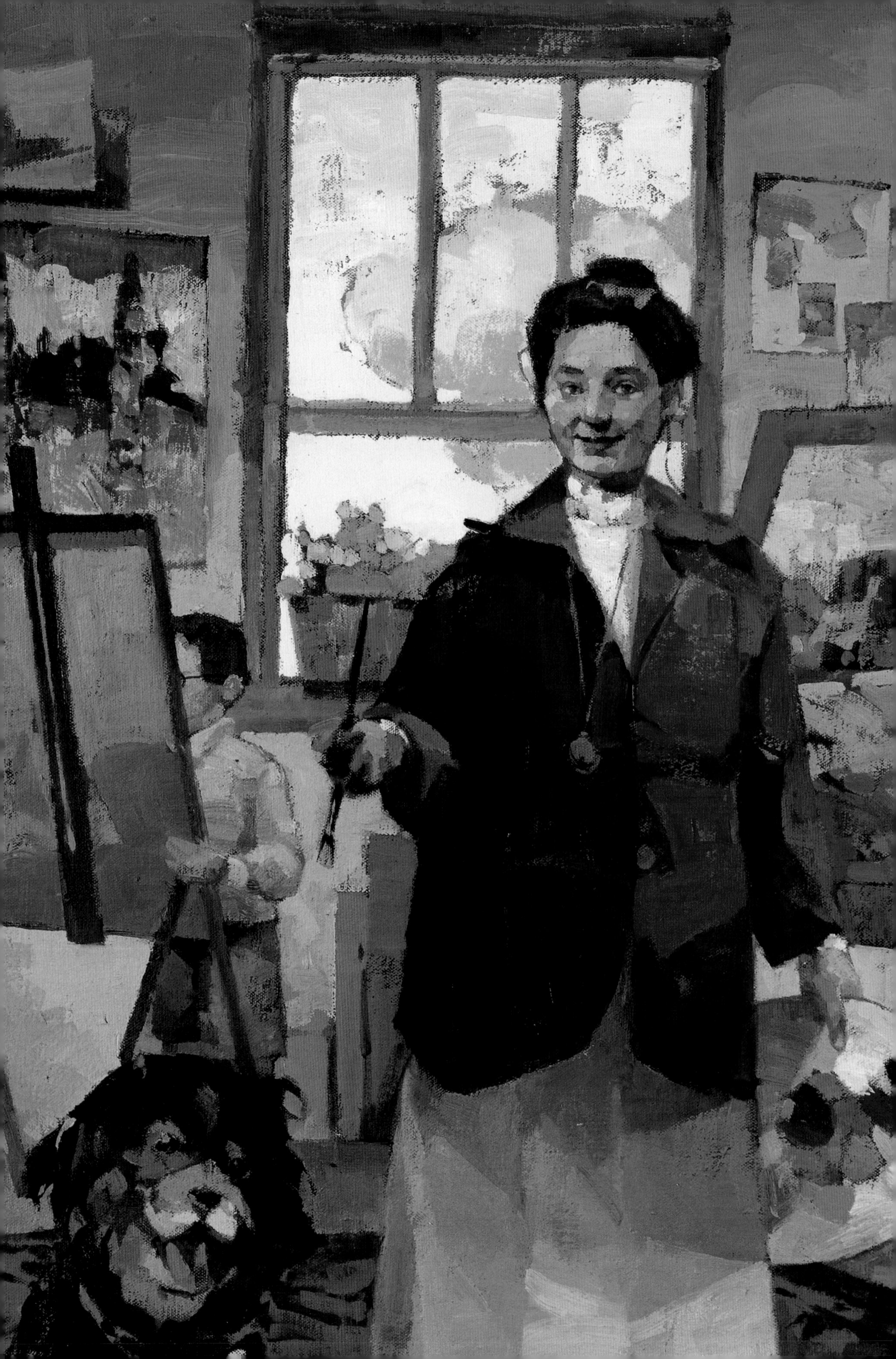

while black-patched Billie
barked and bounded to greet us,

and Miss Carr,
dark hair falling from a pile on her head,
lit up and laughed with us all.

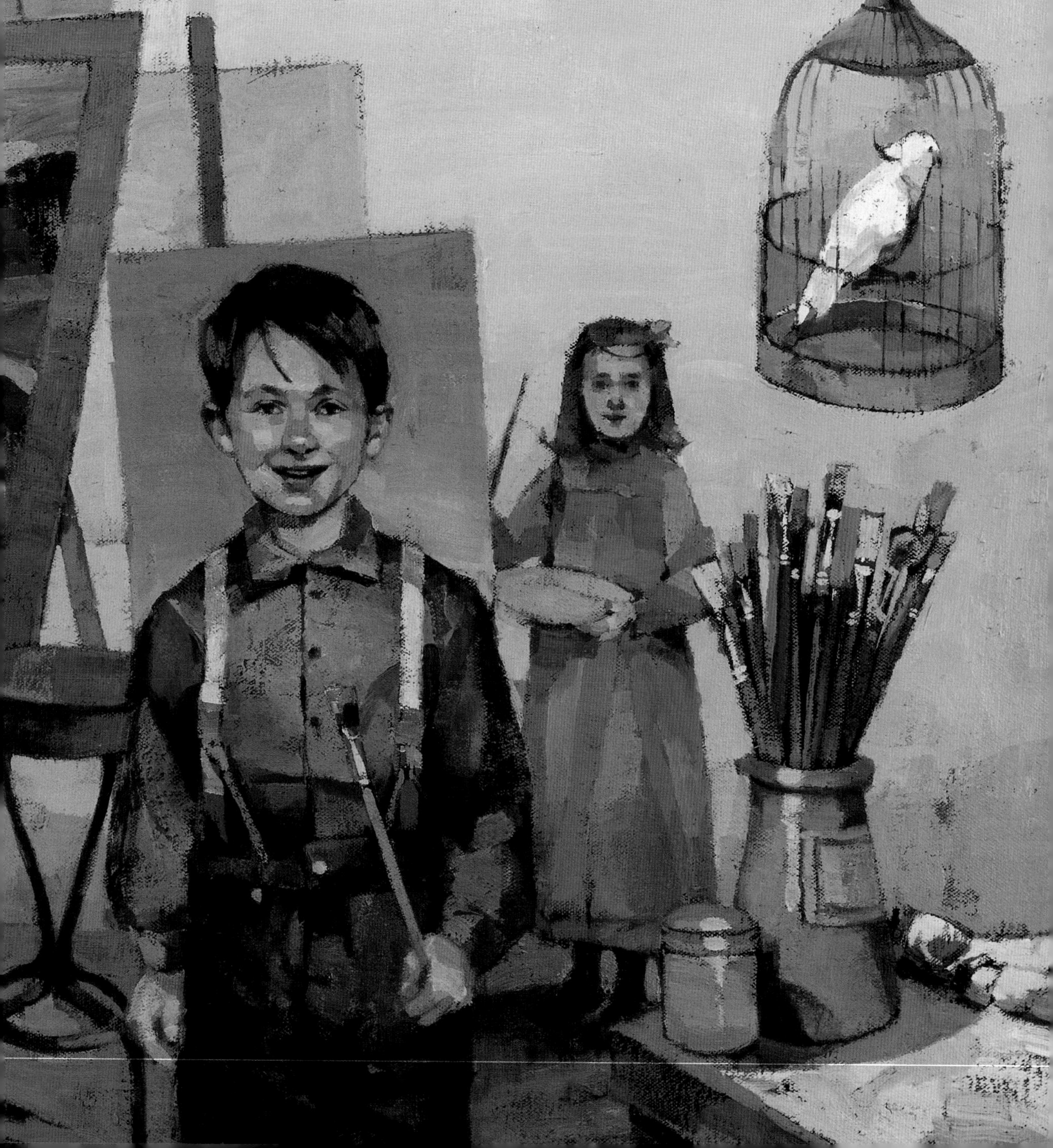

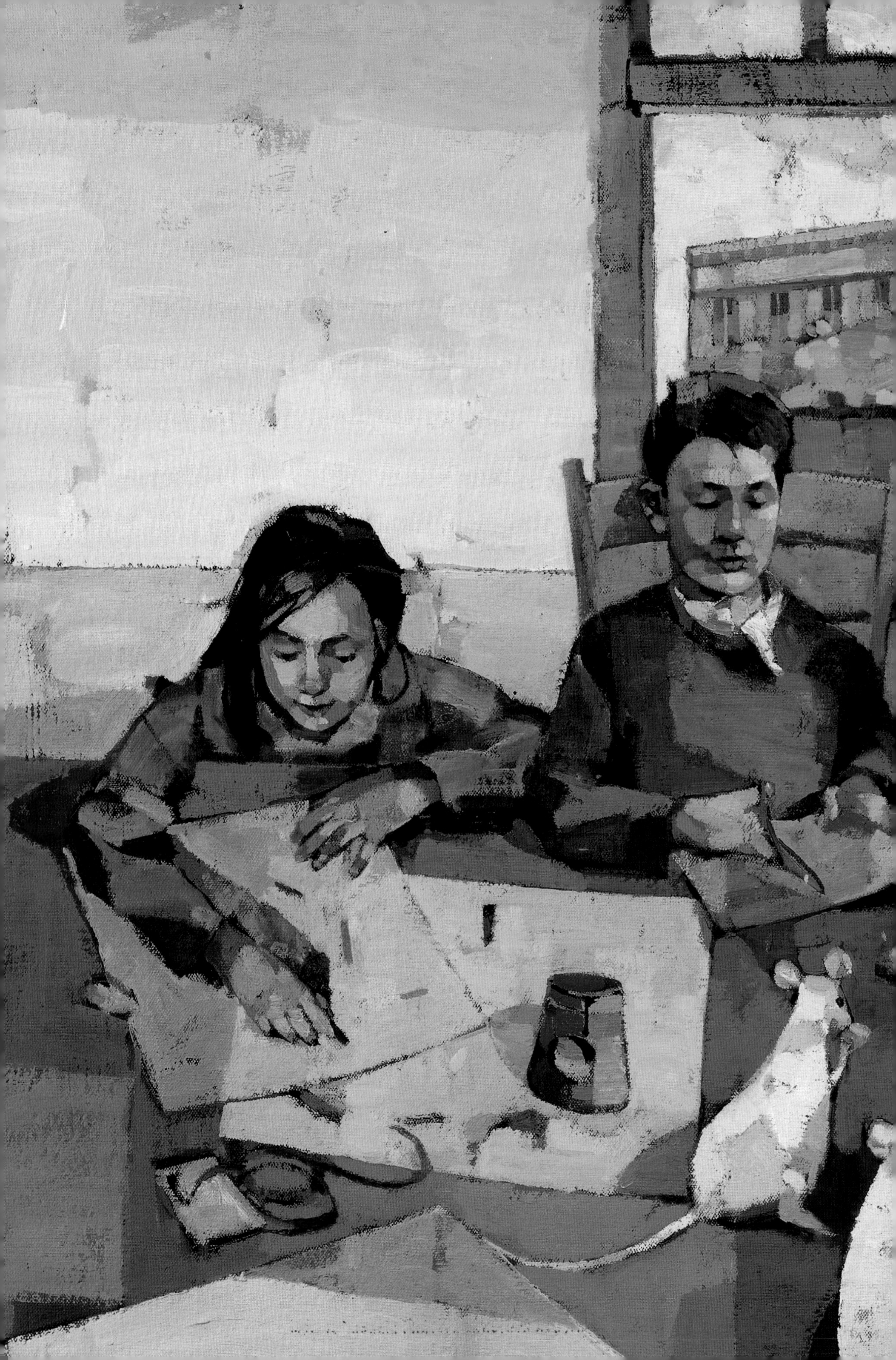

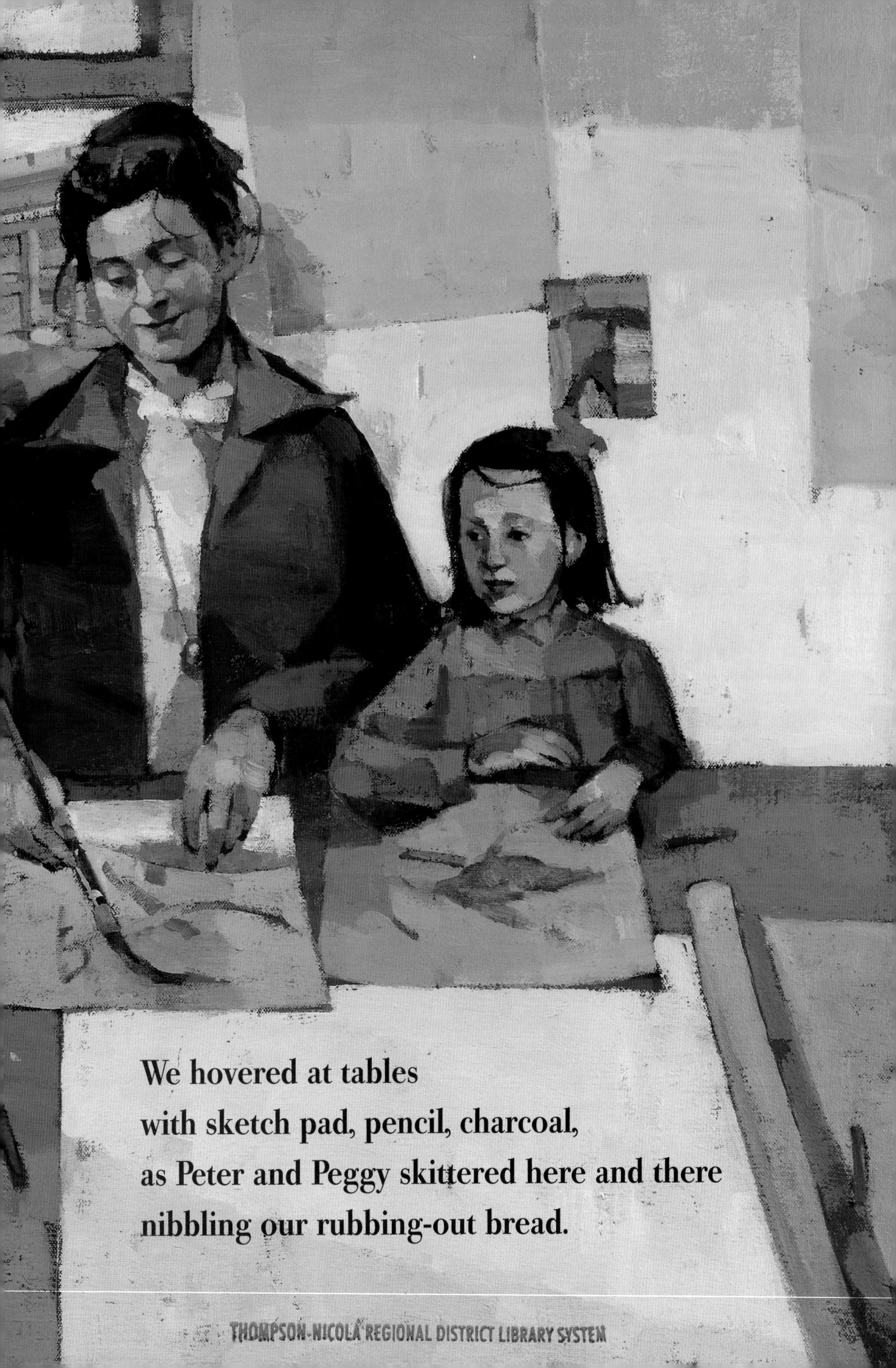

We hovered at tables
with sketch pad, pencil, charcoal,
as Peter and Peggy skittered here and there
nibbling our rubbing-out bread.

We perched on stools
while Sally perched on Miss Carr,
and we copied casts of hands,
heads of friends,
as “our artist” danced and sang
her way through the room,
pointing out, rubbing out,
ahing, naying or demonstrating,
getting us to make paint fly
and paper come alive.

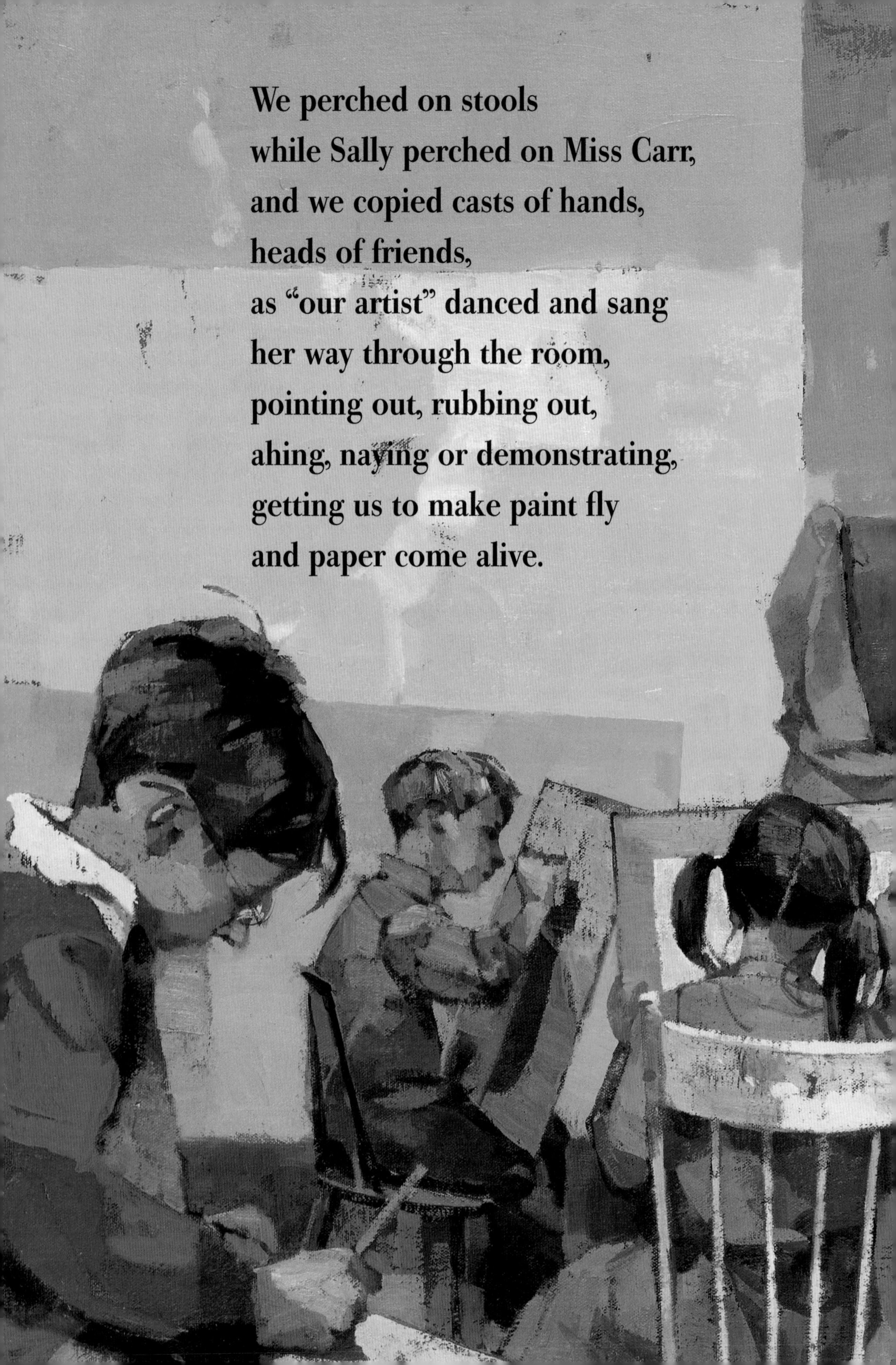

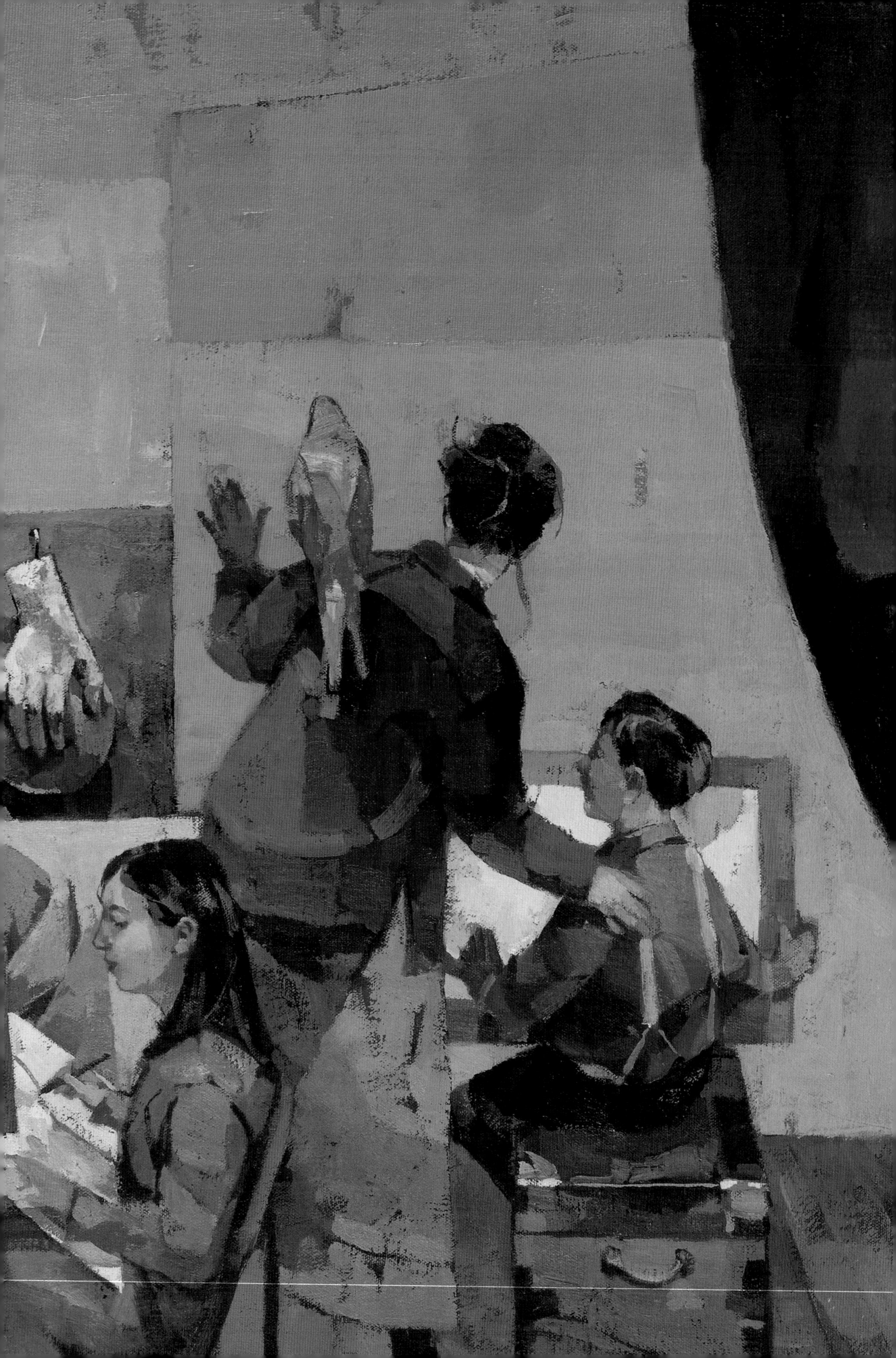

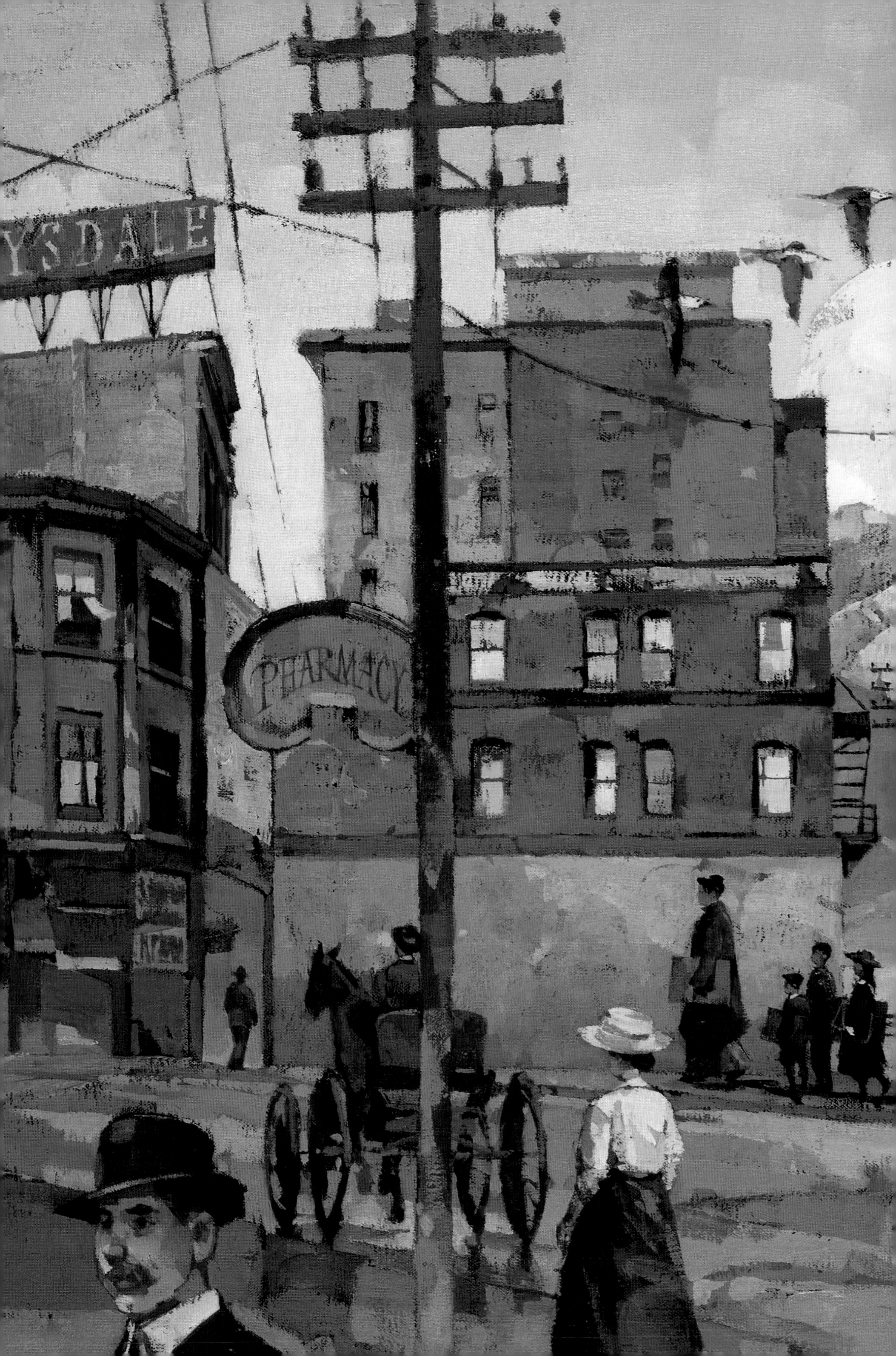
YSDALE
PHARMACY

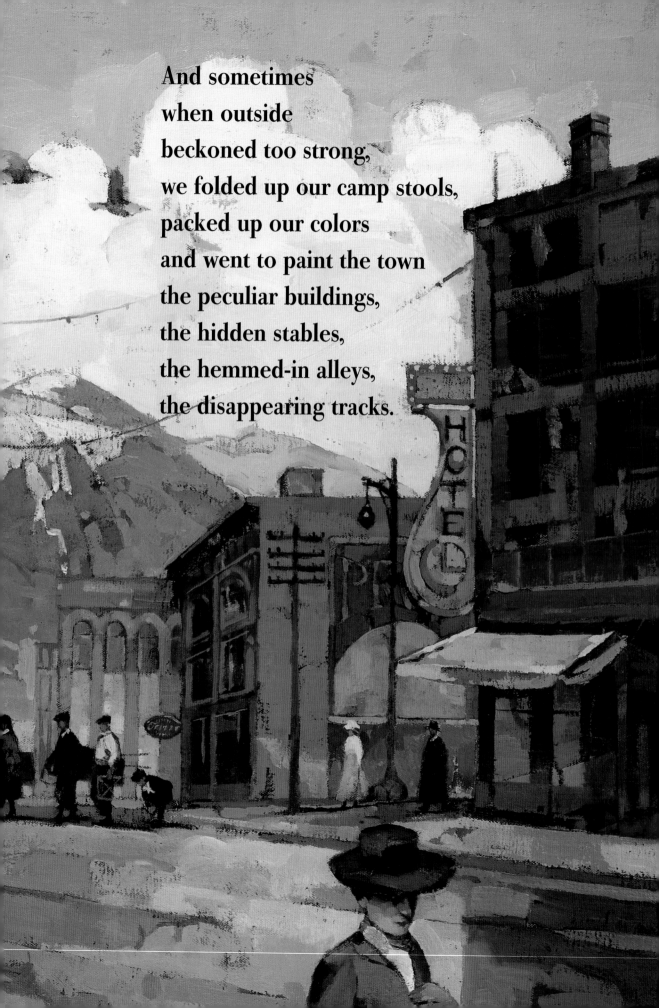

And sometimes
when outside
beckoned too strong,
we folded up our camp stools,
packed up our colors
and went to paint the town
the peculiar buildings,
the hidden stables,
the hemmed-in alleys,
the disappearing tracks.

Or we hoofed it with Billie
across the bridge
and set up our gear
at the edge of the park
to paint, "en plein air,"
the tide-washed inlets,
the plant-hugging banks,
the boat-bobbing harbor.

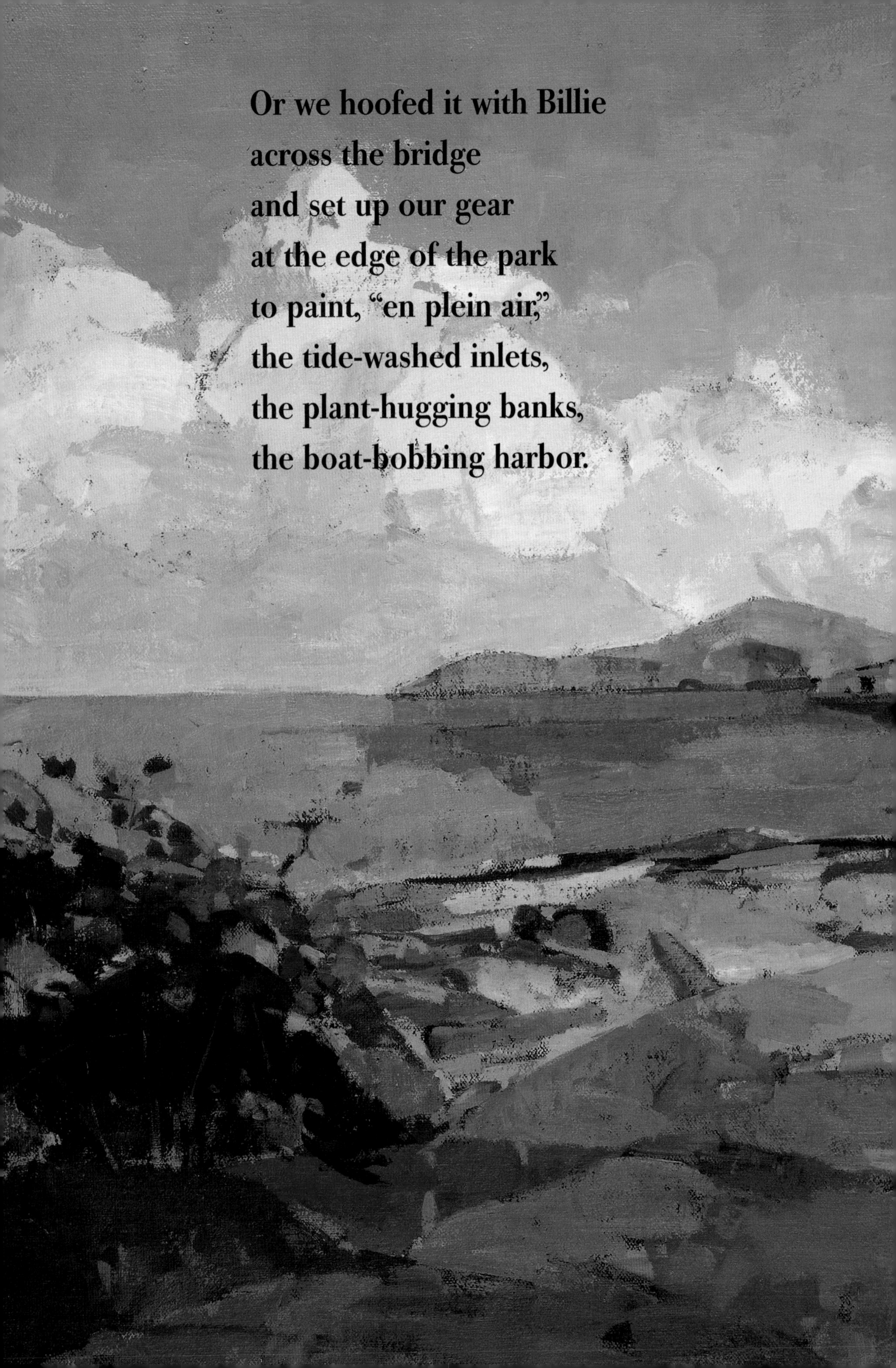

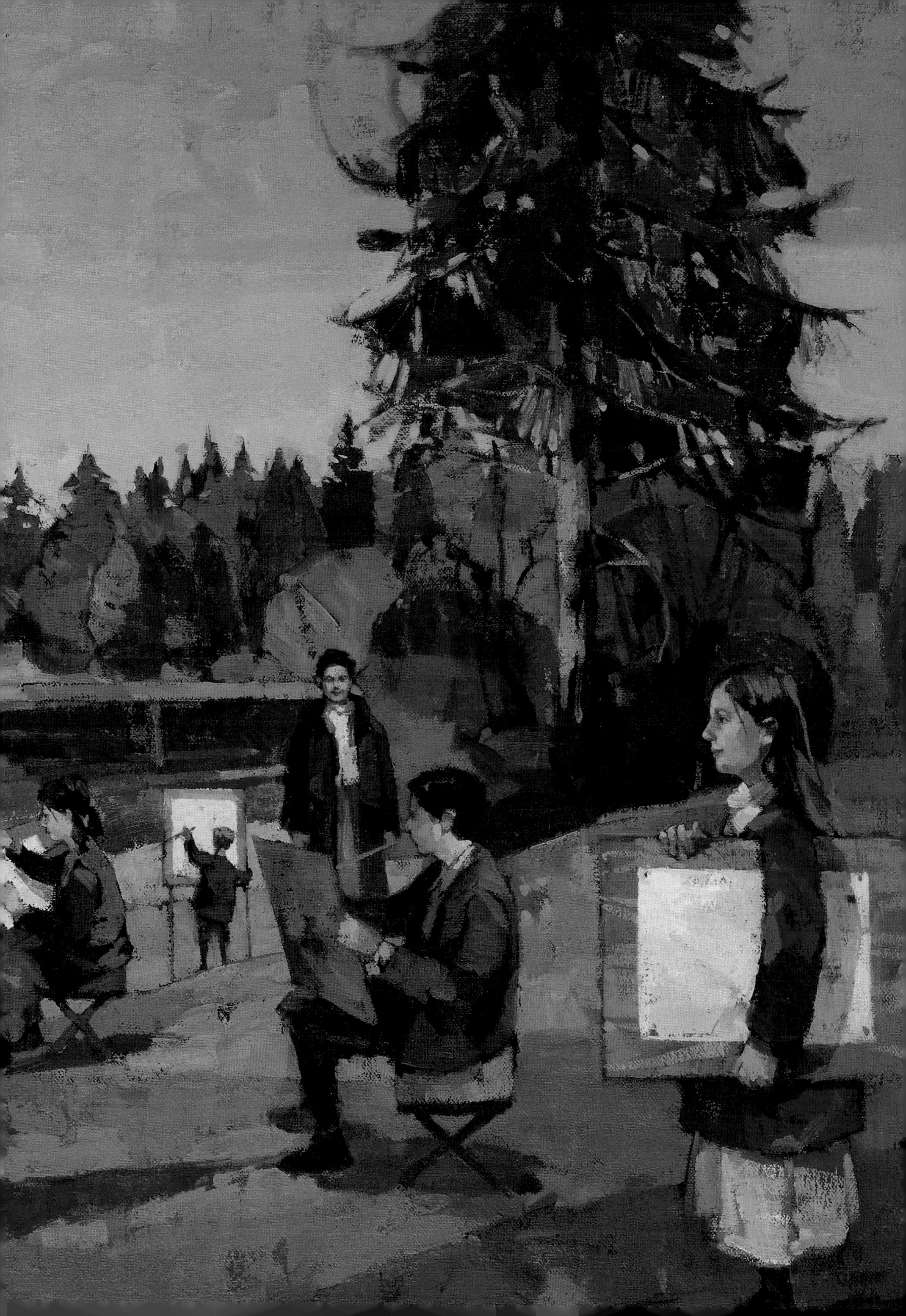

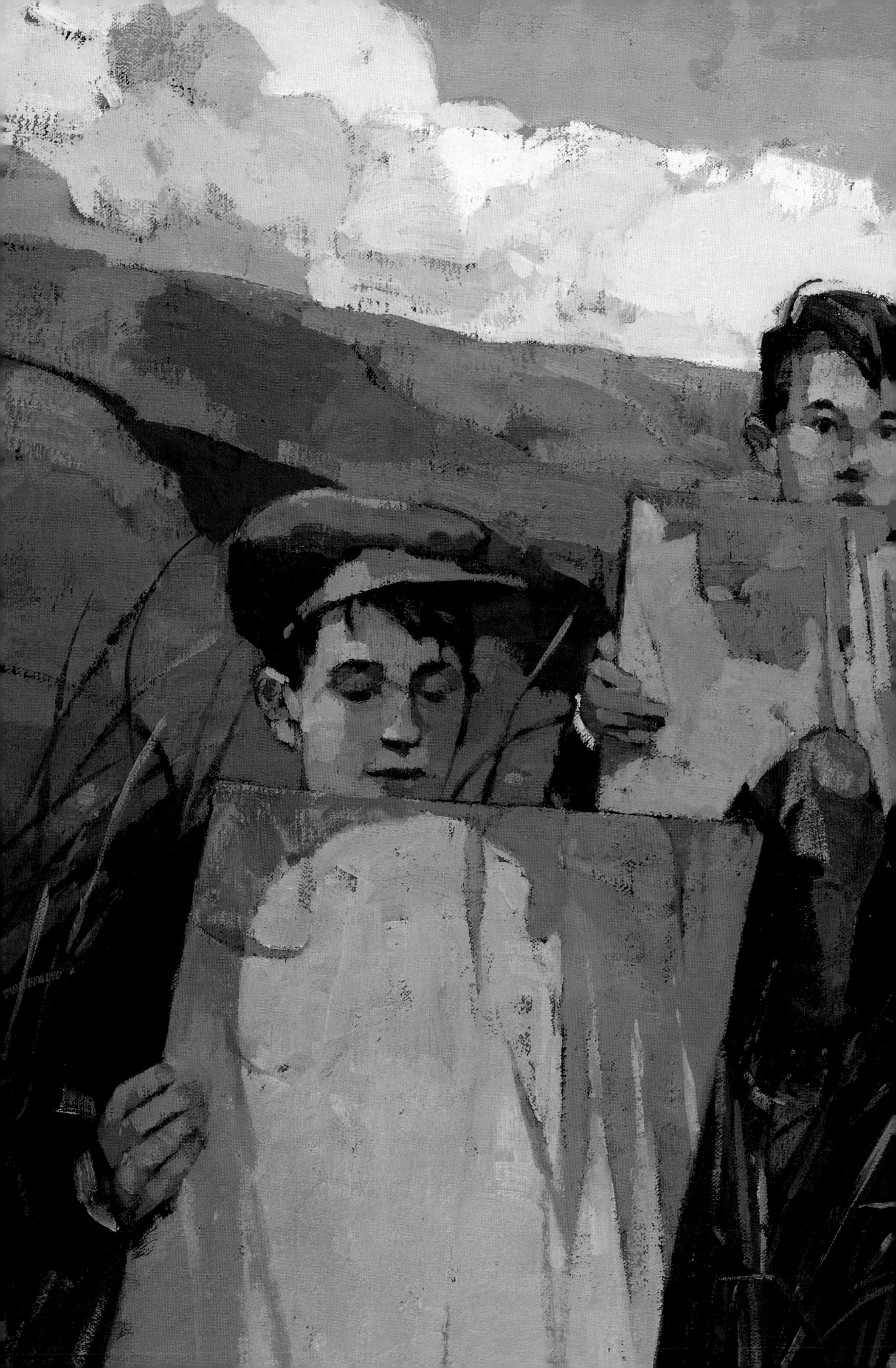

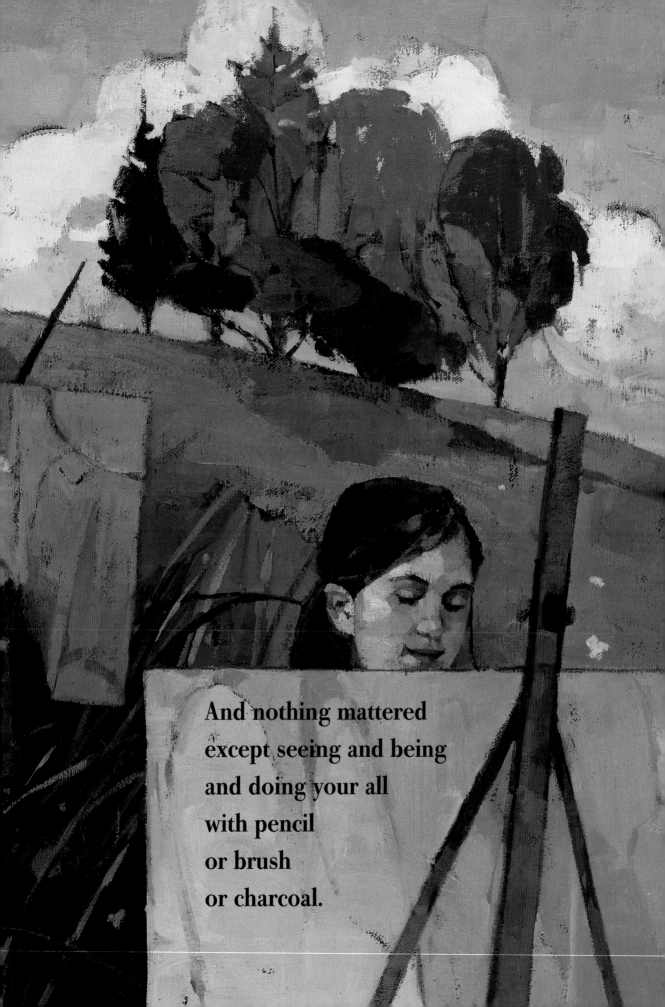

And nothing mattered
except seeing and being
and doing your all
with pencil
or brush
or charcoal.

Back in the studio,
when time was up
and more,
the water was boiled,
the tea slopped out,
and we giggled
and gulped
and gabbed
with Miss Carr
about people, and animals, and art.

Only then did we tear our gaze from
thickening trees,
summer shores,
thunderbird houses,
and drag ourselves
down those hard cold stairs,
past the darkened offices
into the dimming light
of our parents' waiting world.

Oh, we sighed
and waved bye,

and then went out to see
with eyes that were wide.